DEMON TEDDY

NICHOLAS ALLAN

RED FOX

To Amanda

A Red Fox Book

Published by Random House Children's Books
20 Vauxhall Bridge Road, London SW1V 2SA

A division of The Random House Group Ltd
London Melbourne Sydney Auckland
Johannesburg and agencies throughout the world

3 5 7 9 10 8 6 4 2

First published in Great Britain by
Hutchinson Children's Books 1999
Red Fox edition 2000

Printed in Singapore by Tien Wah Press (PTE) Ltd

THE RANDOM HOUSE GROUP Limited Reg. No. 954009
www.randomhouse.co.uk

ISBN 0-09-940761-2

Katie was a shy little girl.

Dominic said she was stupid.

Dominic was a sneaky little boy.
But Miss Bird thought he was perfect.

Katie knew the right answers,
but wasn't always sure...
Dominic was sure of everything.

Katie was often lonely.

One day she bought a wonderful

teddy bear who talked to her.

She took him to school.
Dominic said she was soppy.

That day was Miss Bird's birthday.
She had a new bag.

'Please, Miss Bird,' said Dominic, 'can you show us your new –'

-went Fluffy suddenly, and everyone thought it was Dominic.

The Head gave Miss Bird a huge bunch of flowers.

'Gosh, Miss Bird,' said Dominic, 'you've got a great big –'

-went Fluffy, and everyone thought it was Dominic.

Later Miss Bird asked, 'If a man eats ten cakes and then eats ninety cakes, what would that make?'

'Please, Miss Bird.' Dominic put up his hand. 'It'd make –'

-went Fluffy, and everyone thought it was Dominic.

Dominic didn't dare say another word. So Katie did.

'Well done, Katie,' Miss Bird said.

That afternoon was the school outing.
Katie told some jokes and everyone laughed.

And soon she had

lots of friends.

So Dominic decided, with Fluffy's help, he'd
teach them all a lesson.

Dominic said, 'I think you lot are all a load of –'

ANGELS

-went Fluffy, and everyone thought it was Dominic.
'What a sweet boy,' they said.

When it was time to clear up Miss Bird asked,
'Who's going to help?'

Dominic said, 'I'm not -'

BUSY!

-went Fluffy, and everyone thought it was Dominic.
'Sweet, kind boy,' they all said.

And before long Dominic had some friends too.

But then Katie saw Dominic with Fluffy.
'Give him back,' she cried.
'*No!*' he said.

So she hit him.

-went Fluffy, and
Dominic thought it
was Katie.

-went Fluffy, and
Katie thought it
was Dominic.

So Katie said, 'Will you be my friend?'
And Dominic said, 'Well, all right.'
And Katie said, 'Shall we go and play then?'
And Dominic said, 'Yes, let's go and play.'

And this time Fluffy didn't have to say anything at all.